For Vincent and Eliott

First published in Great Britain in 2009
by Zero To Ten Limited,
part of the Evans Publishing Group,
2A Portman Mansions, Chiltern Street, London W1U 6NR

Printed on chlorine free paper from sustainably managed sources

British Library Cataloguing in Publication Data
Axworthy, Ann
The dragon who couldn't do sporty things
1. Athletic ability - Pictorial works - Juvenile fiction
2. Dragons - Pictorial works - Juvenile fiction
3. Children's stories - Pictorial works
I. Title
823.9'14[J]
ISBN (HB) 9781840895339
ISBN (PB) 9781840895568

Printed in China by WKT Co. Ltd

THE DRAGON WHO COULDN'T DO SPORTY THINGS

written & illustrated by

ANNI AXWORTHY

Little Dragon lived with Jago and his family in a house that had an attic full of ghosts. Each day he waved Jago and his sister off to school, and Mum and Dad off to work. Then Little Dragon made himself a pile of sandwiches and settled in front of the TV until teatime. He knew all the soap stars and could even sing the songs from the adverts.

One evening, as Little Dragon reached for his fourth
helping of pizza, he felt something poke his tummy.
"Have you swallowed a football?" asked Jago.
Little Dragon looked down. He couldn't remember
eating anything that big, so what was it?

"Too much telly and too many
sandwiches, Little Dragon," said Jago's dad.
"I think it's time you had a little exercise," said Jago's mum.

"Come and play football with me," said Jago.

"No! Come and play badminton with me,"
offered Jago's sister.

"I'm going swimming tomorrow.
Why don't you come along?"
said Jago's dad.

"It's my archery class tonight,
you'd love it!" said Jago's mum.

But Little Dragon decided
he wanted a sport of
his very own!

The next morning, before he made his pile of sandwiches and turned on the TV, Little Dragon pulled the phone book from the shelf and opened it at **A**.

"Hmmm... A for athletics club, that sounds fun!"
Little Dragon didn't know what athletics were but clubs are
where you make friends. He phoned the number – the club
was meeting that evening at 5 o'clock.
"Great," thought Little Dragon and headed for the bread bin.

When the family arrived home that evening they
found a note:

The athletics club was not far from home.
There was a small building and lots of grass
with lines drawn on it. A girl ran past in a hurry.
Little Dragon asked a man in a tracksuit
if he could join the club.

"Of course! I'll be your coach. Are you sprints, marathon, triple jump, shot put or javelin?" Little Dragon just stood with his mouth open. "Let's try you out on the running track, shall we?" He led Little Dragon to a white line on the grass and took out a watch. "READY...STEADY...GO!"

Little Dragon ran as fast as he could, until
he reached the place where he had started.
Exhausted, he collapsed in a heap next
to the coach. The coach smiled and said,
"Let's try long jump then, shall we?"

He led Little Dragon to a grassy patch
with a length of sand where
a boy ran and jumped.

Then Little Dragon ran and jumped . . .

"wOWEE!"

Little Dragon landed in the sand –
and started to build a sandcastle! "COME AND HELP!"
he called to the coach who was busy looking up at the clouds.

"What about the shot put?" the coach asked
the now very sandy Little Dragon.
"Just throw this ball as far as you can."
The ball was so heavy that when
Little Dragon lifted it up he
fell over backwards in a heap!

Little Dragon had seen
pictures of ancient warriors
throwing spears.
He'd always wanted
to have a go.

He took hold of the javelin – it felt very heavy. He started to run . . .

The point stabbed into the ground and Little Dragon, holding tightly to the other end, found himself flying through the air . . .

AAAHHHHHHH!

As Little Dragon landed with a bump he heard clapping. The coach rushed over to help him up.

"Ah, I know just the sport for you," said the coach, looking very pleased.

He led Little Dragon to a high pole balanced on two bars.

Little Dragon liked the look of the bouncy mattress on the other side.

"Here, have a go," said the coach, handing Little Dragon another long pole. "Just like you did before."

Little Dragon ran towards the bars. The pole was very long and started to wobble, and then the end got stuck in the ground.

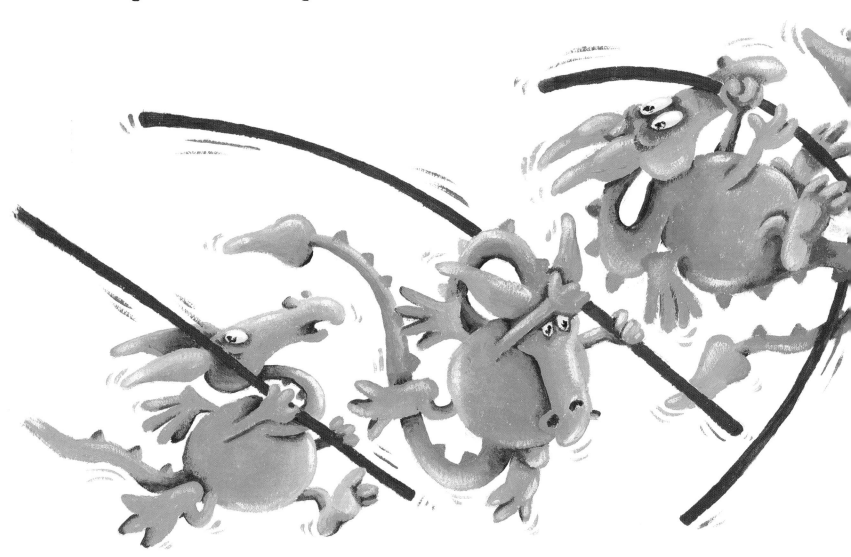

"Oh bother!" said Little Dragon as he felt his feet leave the ground.

Little Dragon felt himself flying through the air,
higher and higher, up over the pole . . .

Finally he bounced on to the big mattress!

"Hurrah!"
The whole club cheered.

Later that summer the athletics club held a big competition. Jago's family watched in amazement each time Little Dragon flew through the air. At the end of the day the coach presented him with a big silver cup. On the side, in big letters, it said LITTLE DRAGON, POLE VAULT CHAMPION.